F.I.F.O.

WHEN THE ALIENS COME FOR YOU, THEY DON'T BRING FLOWERS

GRIVANTE

ART BY
VIKTOR

GRIVANTE PRESS

PART I – THE EXCHANGE

Jack Spaulding stood across the table from the Vulgarian known only as Edgar. That was the closest approximation Jack could make when the alien first gurgled out his name two weeks ago at Haight & Lau, where Jack—ever the low man on the totem pole—had the honor of meeting alien clients.

Edgar's toad-like face glistened under the flickering overhead lights, his bulging eyes scanning the room as he croaked something unintelligible over the thunder of industrial bass reverberating from the concert house below.

"Where... are... they... Jack?" Each word came with a slow, deliberate lurch of Edgar's glistening neck, his rubbery jowls ballooning outward before snapping back. The air between them stank of swamp and rotted meat. Jack tried not to gag.

"My clients are on their way, Edgar. They've got your stuff. Should be here any minute now." His voice cracked. He forced a smile and tugged at his collar, face flushing crimson.

The stuff in question was *Bufo Alvarius* toad venom—one of the strongest natural hallucinogens known to man. But to the Vulgarians, it's a prized aphrodisiac.

Unfortunately, its use usually results in a death or three, and its exportation has been banned by the Galactic Federation due to the carnage it causes. After ingesting the aphrodisiac, the males secrete hormones through pustules on their skin. From there, every Vulgarian they come in contact with is worked into a sexual frenzy until they find release by whatever means necessary.

All natural sources on the Vulgarian home world have been depleted.

"Hope... so...." Edgar turned and looked at his four compatriots, then barked something in their native tongue. One replied, and the four of them stepped their hulking forms back into the shadows of the loft, hands resting on their holstered blaster pistols. Jack's eyes widened, and Edgar spoke again. "Caution... wise..."

"Hey, sure thing, no problem. My clients are stand-up guys. They'll be here in no time. Don't worry." Jack turned away and paced, boots thudding against the wood floor as the thunder of music from below added to his unraveling nerves.

How the hell had Martinez talked him into this? Right. Money. A shot at partner. And maybe—just maybe—if all went well, this could be the start of a lucrative relationship for everyone. If this went sideways, though? He didn't even want to think about what the Vulgarians would do.

He glanced at his watch for the tenth time, palms getting sweatier with each passing second. They were late—but not too late. Not yet. If his clients didn't show soon, the Vulgarians might decide to settle things their own way—and Jack had heard stories that made his balls run and hide. And then there was Megan. He did not want to explain another late night out, even if he had a real excuse this time.

Haight & Lau specialized in murky deals—arranging for certain on-world clients to quietly move goods to off-world buyers like the Vulgarians. The trick was keeping everything smooth and polite, especially when working with species that smelled like wet compost and had a fondness for using plasma rifles as negotiation tools.

A croak from Edgar brought Jack out of his head. He looked up, catching the large, baggy eyes above the alien's flabby jowls tracking his pacing feet. The Vulgarian's tongue hung out, wagging slowly as he watched.

Jack opened his mouth, preparing to offer more assurances on the trustworthiness of his clients, when the knock came at the door. "Ah, good, they're here." Turning on his heels, he walked to the door, muttering under his breath, "Finally."

The door swung open before he'd gotten halfway there. Two men stepped in, Tommy guns held at waist height, fingers on the triggers. Jack screamed and dove for safety. Short flashes of white trembled in the air, followed by darkness as something hit him over the head and the music from below faded away.

PART II - PROBING QUESTIONS

Jack surfaced into groggy awareness, eyelids crusted shut and muscles aching like he'd been trampled. A cold slab pressed against his spine—concrete? Metal? Wherever he was, it wasn't the loft.

He tried to move, but nothing obeyed. Panic flared. His arms, chest, and legs were pinned tight—strapped down.

"What the hell...?" His voice rasped in the stale air. Dim lights glowed overhead, casting strange shadows. Then a face leaned into view. Edgar.

"Hey—Edgar—I didn't know they were going to stiff you, okay? That wasn't part of the deal," Jack croaked, his voice cracking with panic.

Edgar let out a series of wet chortles, his jowls trembling like gelatin. "...was... funny..."

"Funny?" Jack squinted upward, bile rising in his throat. "So, what's the punchline? Why am I strapped to a table?"

Edgar reached into a pouch at his hip and pulled out a drool-slicked device. Jack recognized it instantly: a Translaphone. Round top, square base—but how it hadn't short-circuited with all that goo on it, Jack didn't know.

Edgar brought the Translaphone to his jowls and barked a stream of wet, guttural syllables into it, splattering it with even more slime. A speaker near Jack's head crackled, translating in a twangy Ozark drawl:

"You shoulda chose better partners, boy. You're foolishness amuses us."

Jack's throat tightened. "Wait—Edgar—what are you going to do to me?"

The Vulgarian didn't answer right away. Instead, he turned and rummaged below the table. When he rose again, he held a long, dark, glistening tube in one hand.

"What all aliens do when they abduct a human."

A door across the chamber hissed open, flooding the room with cold air and a jarring light. Jack flinched, the chill crawling across his bare legs. That's when he realized—no pants.

"What the fuck!" he shouted. "You're going to probe me?"

Edgar spoke into the Translaphone again. The voice that came back through the speaker oozed hillbilly menace:

"That's usually how we start. Pig fucker."

Edgar waddled to the end of the table and grabbed a crank hidden beneath a panel. With each turn, metal chains groaned overhead, tugging Jack's feet up and apart like he was a chicken being prepped for rotisserie. Cold air hit new, vulnerable bits.

Leather straps cinched tighter around his ankles. Edgar's face reappeared—between Jack's legs this time—his eyes wide with what might've been clinical focus… or twisted lust.

"Wait—Edgar—listen, we can talk about this. There's no need to— AAHHH!"

The probe plunged in with a sickening squelch. Jack's entire spine spasmed. Eyes rolled back. Nerves lit up like a thousand points of light before everything went black again.

Jack was starting to think he preferred the darkness.

PART III – WAITING IN THE QUEUE

"Whose... next?" are the first words Jack heard upon awakening.

He blinked, vision swimming. His head throbbed. His stomach twisted, then erupted. He turned just in time to vomit a hot stream across the floor, pain lighting up every nerve from gut to throat.

As his eyes cleared, he looked down the length of his body. A different Vulgarian stood between his spread legs, adjusting something beneath the table.

He groaned and quickly swiveled his head to the side, hoping for darkness but settling for something else to focus on. Across the dim chamber, Edgar lounged with another of his kind, sipping a drink and puffing on some kind of glowing smoking stick. They noticed Jack and raised their glasses in a silent toast, paired with a grotesque curving of fleshy jowls.

Jack rolled his head the other way, trying to tune it all out—but his eyes caught something worse. Along the far wall, a line of Vulgarians stood in eerie silence, tongues lolling and jowls twitching in anticipation.

There weren't just a few. At least ten. Maybe more. Their forms blurred together in the dimness, each hulking figure stepping forward as the last one finished.

He followed the line until he was staring into the next set of beady alien eyes looming between his legs.

"Fuck."

The world went dark again, and Jack welcomed the void.

————

When light next fell into his opening eyes, Jack found himself sitting up, wrapped in a blanket. He sat in the back of a Vulgarian landing craft, an unwelcome raw soreness between his legs and his clothes in a pile next to him. Across the aisle, Edgar—still with raised jowls in a joker's smile—sat next to two large barrels.

"Where are we?"

"Taking... home..."

"My home..." Jack hesitated. "You're letting me go?"

"Yes... we... are... done."

Done? Jack's heart pounded. "What did you do to me?"

"Taught... lesson."

Raising his brow, Jack asked, "What lesson?"

Edgar grabbed a Translaphone from the wall behind him.

"Don't screw with the Vulgarians."

"Or?" Jack asked automatically, still confused.

Edgar didn't answer.

"What about the Colombians?"

Edgar motioned toward the large barrels beside him with a twist of his head that left his jowls bouncing, drool splashing onto the floor.

PART IV - HOME AGAIN

Two weeks later.

Megan purred into Jack's ear as she climbed atop him, hand wrapping around his neck and pulling him to her.

"C'mon, honey. Let's forget the world for a while."

Jack flinched beneath her, hands moving to her shoulders with a gentle push off of him.

"Megan, don't."

He avoided her eyes, staring blankly at the flickering TV screen as if the latest political scandal held some grand impact on his life—or at least a decent excuse for his behavior.

He couldn't tell her the truth. Hell, he couldn't even say it out loud to himself. Maybe it was just stress. A residual trauma response. His mind kept clinging to that idea like a shield—because the alternative was unthinkable. How do you talk about something that rewired your body and made your skin crawl at the thought of touch?

Megan eased off him, hurt flickering across her face before she masked it with a forced smile.

"It's been weeks, Jack. Are you sure everything's okay?"

She sat back, watching him with eyes that weren't accusing—just tired, and maybe a little scared. The silence between them wasn't just physical anymore. It was turning into something that had weight.

Megan's voice tightened, coming out as if she were choking.

"Jack, are you—" she coughed on her own spittle, "—having an affair?"

Jack's head snapped around.

"What? No. God, no. You know me better than that."

She stared at him for a long moment.

"Then what is it?"

He opened his mouth, then his eyes trembled and he closed it.

Not wanting to let the moment pass, she pushed.

"I know I've changed since we had Katie, but this isn't about me, Jack. You're not just tired. You're haunted. And you won't let me in. Lately it's like you don't even know I exist, ever since that night you didn't come home. I feel alone."

Jack looked down, blinking the moisture in his eyes away. He didn't have a lie ready. And the truth? That wasn't coming out. He bit the side of his cheek.

"It's not you, honey," he managed, offering her an unconvincing smile. "I promise."

Megan sat in the silence that followed, her hands folded tightly in her lap. She wanted to believe him—needed to—but the way his voice had cracked, the way his body recoiled from her touch... it didn't feel like the man she knew.

Still, she leaned in. Gently, she touched his cheek.

"Whatever this is, Jack... you don't have to face it alone. I'm here."

He didn't answer. Couldn't. The lump in his throat would drown him if he even opened his mouth.

Megan tried not to take it personally. But deep down, she felt something slipping. And she didn't know how to stop it.

"The next deal will be better," she murmured, brushing her lips against his temple. "You'll make partner. I know you will. Another big deal will be coming your way."

She kissed his cheeks as warm tears fell, whispering sweet encouraging words.

Jack moved before he even realized it, needing to take action and get out of his thoughts. He kissed her—slow at first, then more urgently.

She responded, wrapping herself around him with a hopeful sigh.

Megan found herself on her back, Jack above her, his breath ragged against her skin. She closed her eyes and let her mind drift. It wasn't what she had in mind, but maybe this was how it needed to start—slowly, awkwardly, imperfect.

———

Her mind wandered.

Maybe if they got lucky, she'd get pregnant again. After all, Katie's almost four. It's time for the next one. She really wanted three or four kids, but Jack kept insisting they take it slow until he made partner. That reminded her—she'd have to call his secretary at the firm and thank her for letting her know about the deal falling apart at the last minute. Jack may never have talked about it otherwise.

Men.

Oh, and she should probably go by the store and pick up some—

———

For Jack, the act felt mechanical. He was willing to do anything to stop her questions. He focused on her warmth, the way her hands moved over his back, her quiet gasps—anything to anchor himself in the now and not in that cold, alien room.

But the pressure was building. Not just physical. Something inside him turned over—sharp and wrong. His gut twisted.

He buried his face in the pillow next to her and grunted through clenched teeth.

"Almost there."

Here we go, she thought, and murmured something soft, encouraging. Her voice felt far away.

Then it hit him—pain and pressure exploding outward from deep inside. His body spasmed.

He rolled off her with a groan and curled into himself, trembling.

Megan lay still beside him, staring at his back, her heart thudding dully against her ribs.

That wasn't what she expected. Not from Jack. Not from tonight.

He'd needed something. But whatever it was, it hadn't been her. Not really.

She turned to him slowly, watching as he curled tighter, his body trembling like his body was about to collapse in on itself. His hands clutched at his belly.

"Jack?" she whispered, but he didn't respond.

She wanted to reach for him, to pull him into her arms like she used to when he came home defeated or exhausted. But now, he looked... afraid.

Of what, she didn't know.

Maybe of her.

Or maybe of himself.

She lay back down, staring up at the ceiling and blinking away tears. She wasn't sure who she was more scared for—Jack, or their future.

"It hurts," he groaned.

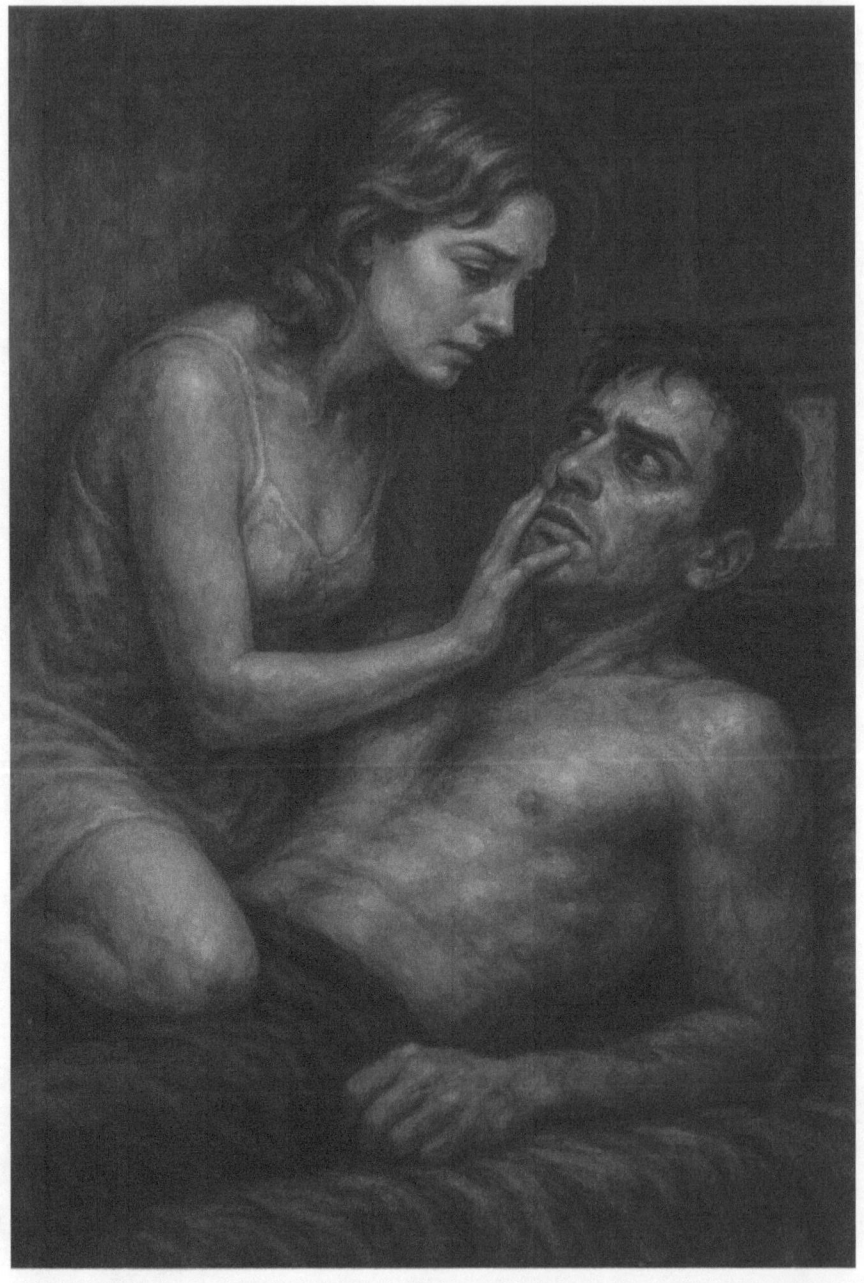

PART V – MAKING BABIES

J ack sat rigid in the plastic lobby chair, one leg bouncing uncontrollably. Megan held his hand, but he barely registered the warmth—his mind kept replaying last night in a loop of pain, confusion, and shame.

Megan squeezed his fingers. "You're going to be okay," she whispered—not sure who needed convincing more.

Across the room, a kid coughed. A receptionist answered the phone. Everything felt too normal.

When the nurse finally appeared and called their last name, both stood slowly. Their fingers stayed laced as they walked, Jack's squeezing tight enough to hurt her, but she grit her teeth instead of speaking up.

———

The doctor's office was cold and too quiet. Jack sat hunched on the edge of the chair, Megan's hand gripping his tight, offering comfort, reassurance, presence.

Dr. Jones entered with a polite nod, but his expression didn't match the usual rehearsed calm. He avoided eye contact as he slid the x-ray films onto the view box and flipped on the light.

A strange white mass with tendrils branching out glowed on the film, like something foreign squatting behind Jack's guts.

"Jack. Megan." The doctor finally looked up. "I have... well, I'm not entirely sure in situations like this the best way to proceed."

Megan straightened in her seat. Jack didn't move.

"Would you rather hear the good news or the bad news first?" Dr. Jones asked, clearly stalling.

They shared a glance and squeezed each other's hands. Then Jack answered, "Let's start with the bad."

Dr. Jones nodded and turned, tapping the glowing mass on the film with the back of his pen. "This... this is what we found."

Jack squinted at the image. It looked like a white blob, with spidery tendrils stretching out in all directions.

"Oh god," Jack muttered. "I've got cancer, don't I?"

"No, it's not cancer," Dr. Jones said quickly. "At least, not any kind we've ever seen. There are no signs of typical malignancy. No cellular breakdown. If anything..." he shifted in his seat, "based on what you told me about the pain you experienced during climax—how something felt restricted—a tumor is the best we could label it, but it appears to be... functioning." He leaned closer to the screen, eyes narrowing with a mix of wonder and confusion. "It's responding to your physiology in real-time."

"Functioning?" Megan echoed, her mouth falling open. "Like... alive? What is it?"

The doctor didn't answer at first. He just looked at Jack. And for the first time since they'd walked in, Jack saw something new in the doctor's eyes: fear.

Jack leaned forward, voice hoarse. "You're telling me there's something alive inside me?"

Dr. Jones adjusted his glasses and nodded slowly. "In a manner of speaking... yes. It's not behaving like any tumor I've ever seen. There's no immune response. It's almost like your body... accepted it."

"Accepted it?" Jack barked. "What does that even mean?"

Megan gripped his arm. "What can we do? Is it dangerous? Can it be removed?"

"It's… interfacing with your reproductive system. Tendrils branching into the prostate, testes…" he indicated different spots with his pen. He paused, blinking at the complexity on the scan. "It's structured… but I hesitate to call it engineered. It could be a mutation. A response to some unknown environmental trigger."

Jack pulled his hand away from Megan as his heart skipped a beat and blinked blankly at the doctor. Megan turned a worried expression his way, trying to catch his eye.

"Jack," she asked hesitantly, "what is it?"

After a moment of silence, as Jack continued to blink, Dr. Jones interrupted.

"Jack!" He looked up, eyes watering but appearing to focus at the doctor barking his name.

"I have to ask you: has anything happened to you lately? Any kind of trauma, any unexplained blackouts or memory loss?"

Jack could feel Megan's gaze upon him. His stomach flipped and he pressed a palm to his lower abdomen, half expecting to feel something slither.

"I want it out," he said, his voice low and firm. "Whatever it is. Get it out."

He stood abruptly, then sat back down just as fast, head in his hands.

"Jesus Christ," he whispered. "This isn't real. This can't be real." Maybe it was a hormone imbalance. Maybe the pain, the swelling, the flashes of heat—all of it—could be explained by something… earthly. He wanted to believe that. Needed to.

Dr. Jones said nothing. But his gaze had shifted. No longer as concerned, no longer merely clinical—he looked at Jack like a riddle he desperately wanted to solve.

Megan moved to his side, her hand resting on his back. "Jack…"

He jerked away from her touch—not violently, but enough.

"I didn't ask for this," he snapped. "I didn't do anything to deserve this."

"Jack," Megan said again, quieter now, "we'll figure it out. Okay? We'll get through it."

But Jack was already shaking his head, eyes locked on the x-ray. "I've got something living inside me. Feeding off me. Like I'm some kind of host."

His voice cracked, raw and broken. "What the hell is happening to me?"

Megan opened her mouth to respond but no words came. She looked at Jack—really looked at him—and for a moment, he was a stranger. Pale. Sweating. Haunted.

"Jack..." she said, voice fragile, hand reaching out for his. "How did this happen?"

But he didn't answer. He just kept staring at the x-ray like the heat from his gaze would burn the mass away.

Megan wiped at her eyes, trying to stay strong. But something inside her wobbled.

She turned to Dr. Jones, her voice sharper than she meant it to be. "So what do we do now? You said it's... engineered? Is there a specialist we can talk to? Someone who's dealt with anything like this before?"

Dr. Jones's eyes flicked from Jack to the scan, then back. "I'll make some calls," he said—but his voice lacked conviction.

Jack lurched forward, grabbing a small trash can next to the doctor's desk and vomiting.

"Honey?" Megan cried out next to him.

He glanced up at the doctor, ignoring her. "You said there was good news?"

"Jack?" Megan tried again, tugging on his arm to get his attention.

He glared straight ahead, spitting a string of vomit from his lips. "I don't want to talk about it. Please—the good news?"

Dr. Jones nodded and switched off the image of the x-ray. He tried on a smile that aimed for compassion but came off maniacal as he turned to Megan.

"You're pregnant."

PART VI – TOO HOT TO HANDLE

Jack sat at his desk, staring at the phone like it might ring again and tell him it was all a joke. His hands wouldn't stop shaking. The muscles in his jaw were clenched so tightly it hurt to breathe.

Edgar had finally answered his message routed via the Vulgarian ambassador, but the answer hadn't brought clarity. It had only confirmed his worst suspicion: the thing inside him wasn't done.

He ran a trembling hand across his belly. It felt firmer now, rounded. Not fat—bloated.

It took three years to get that answer, and during that time, Megan gave birth to their second child, Max, now two, and she was amazingly pregnant again. Amazing because during those two years they only had sex to completion twice. The pain that accompanied sexual release for Jack never lessened, so it was rare that he couldn't stop himself.

He could feel it afterward, shifting inside like a satisfied parasite. The x-rays revealed that the mass inside him continued to grow after each orgasm, and now he knew why. Not a kick. A squirm. Like it didn't know how to be born—only how to burrow. Sometimes, in the quietest moments, he swore he could feel it pulsing in rhythm with his heart.

He called Dr. Jones and told him what he had learned. Surgery was highly risky but possible, the doctor had told him—but unfortunately, it would leave Jack without any sexual function whatsoever. Something his ego wouldn't even consider.

Jack grabbed his coat from the rack, fumbling with the sleeves as he tried to shove his arms through. He was sweating again. He couldn't sit here any longer—not after that call, not with this thing growing inside him like a countdown ticking louder by the hour.

He opened his door and leaned out, his voice harsher than he intended. "Mabel. Call Megan. Tell her to meet me at Dr. Jones's office. Now."

Mabel looked up from her desk, her brows knitting together. "Is everything alright, Mr. Spaulding?"

He didn't have it in him to lie—not right now—so he just nodded and started down the hall.

"Um, yes sir," the elderly secretary replied. "But what about your appointment?" She motioned toward the waiting area where a shapely blonde in a tight red dress eyed him.

What the hell? It's bad enough my wife suspects me of having a mistress given the state of our sex life. She'd already demanded I have the oldest secretary at the firm—now I'm going to have to start turning away clients. Why do they always seem to look like that?

"Crap, Mabel. I'm sorry. Please apologize for me and send her over to Henderson."

"Yes, sir. And what about your four o'clock?"

"Who is it?"

"Another new client. A Falun, name is Abigail Sparrow." She looked to the schedule book for a moment. "Needs help setting up an on-world business venture."

"An off-worlder? Hmm..." Jack admired the beauty in the lobby a moment, then leaned across the desk, whispering, "I'll tell you what—if she looks anything like that blonde out there, give her to Henderson as well. If she's old or just ugly, reschedule her for Tuesday with my apologies."

Mabel's mouth fell open and she leaned back. "Well, I never..."

"Please, Mabel. Work with me on this."

PART VII – DO YOU REALLY WANT TO KNOW?

Jack sat stiffly on the exam table, hands clenched at his sides, eyes locked on the floor. His skin itched, his stomach churned, and his pants were doing nothing to hide the now-constant state of arousal that had overtaken his body. It was like being thirteen again—erections at all the wrong times, without warning, without invitation. Only now, the stakes were so much worse.

Megan paced the small room. "You're scaring me, Jack. You said there was an update. What's going on?"

Dr. Jones entered a moment later, clipboard in hand, saving him momentarily. He didn't sit. His gaze flicked to Jack's midsection, then back to his chart.

Jack didn't wait. "Tell her," he muttered.

The doctor cleared his throat. "The mass is growing. Faster now. And… it's not just feeding on Jack's body. It's altering it. Stimulating hormone production—aggressively. Testosterone. Seminal activity."

Megan's brow furrowed. "Wait… what does that mean?"

Jack finally looked up. "It means I'm walking around with a hard-on like I'm a goddamn teenager. Constantly. And if I let myself finish —" he gestured toward his belly, "—this thing gets bigger. Stronger."

Megan's hand flew to her mouth.

Dr. Jones stepped in again, quieter. "It's using your body's arousal as fuel. Sexual stimulus seems to accelerate the developmental cycle."

Megan backed up a step, as if the air between them had shifted. "So, what—if you get turned on, it grows? Like some kind of... parasite with a sex drive?"

"It's not mine," Jack muttered. "It's hijacking me. My body just—reacts. Like I'm stuck in puberty. I can't turn it off. But I have to finish for it to get what it needs."

He shifted uncomfortably on the table, pants clearly tighter than when he'd walked in. "Every time I even think about something... it responds. Sometimes it triggers it. Sometimes it wants it."

Dr. Jones glanced between them. "This isn't just hormonal. There's a feedback loop—psychological, maybe even neurological. The organism knows how to get what it wants."

Megan's voice dropped to a whisper. "Jesus, Jack... it's not just growing inside you. It's taking over."

Megan's arms crossed over her belly, unconsciously at first. She felt the smallest flutter—normal, probably—but her mind refused to let it go.

What if?

She blinked, forcing herself to breathe. No. That was fear talking. Paranoia.

Still, her hand lingered there, protective and suddenly unsure.

Jack saw the gesture—and it broke him.

"There's more," he said.

Dr. Jones raised an eyebrow. "More?"

Jack took a shaky breath. "A few years ago... the deal with the Vulgarians. The one that went sideways."

Megan blinked. "You mean the night you didn't come home?"

Jack nodded. "They took me. I woke up on one of their ships. Strapped to a table. They... experimented. Probed me. Over and over. I blacked out for most of it, but it went on for hours. Felt like days. A dozen Vulgarians, maybe more."

Megan's face paled. "Oh my god..."

Jack continued, voice brittle. "That's when it started. After I got back. After the first time we had sex. That's when I noticed something was wrong."

He turned to Dr. Jones. "I reached out to the Vulgarian embassy. Tracked down Edgar—the one I dealt with. He's a captain of one of their merchant vessels that transports goods between their home world and Earth. I finally got a response."

"What did they say?" the doctor asked.

Jack closed his eyes. "First, that he was surprised I hadn't succumbed yet. They impregnated me. They implant their eggs into host bodies. The egg ties itself into our reproductive systems and feeds off chemicals released during orgasm. It takes about ten to twelve feedings before the baby becomes viable."

"Oh god." Megan stumbled backward into the wall, her hand now clutching her belly as she stared down, her face hidden by her dark curly hair—but the choking sobs shook the room. She didn't know if it was the fear of what Jack had become—or the growing certainty that the child inside her might not be hers at all. Not really.

When she finally quieted down, now sitting on the floor, the men broke from their shock.

"How many orgasms have you had, Jack?" Dr. Jones asked.

"Only four."

"Did this Edgar tell you anything else? Did they say it could be removed?"

"Yes and no," Jack said, shaking his head, wincing as his wife's body heaved with fresh sobs.

She looked up at him, wiping the wetness away and smearing her makeup. "What else?"

He took a deep breath. "The man at the embassy said the egg… it alters the host's DNA. My sperm. I'm not sure how to describe it but any of my offspring are potential hosts too. It passes on the other eggs."

Megan stared at him, frozen. Then her face cracked.

"You mean Max? And the baby?" Her voice broke on the last word and she struggled to her feet. They were hers. Weren't they? But now... she wasn't sure if she was a mother or just another vessel. A nursery borrowed by something else.

Jack could only nod. "I didn't know. I swear. Not until today."

She flung the door open and ran from the room. Not just from Jack. From the truth that had already begun to twist her love into suspicion.

"I didn't know!" he called after the fleeing form of his wife.

PART VIII – LUNCH DATE?

Papers cluttered Jack's desk like fallen leaves—messy, brown, dead. He didn't care. His eyes locked on the photo in the center: Megan and the kids. Katie. Max. And little Molly, who wouldn't remember any of this.

Molly's second birthday was coming up. She was healthy, at least by every measurable standard. Unless you counted the alien parasite curled quietly in her insides.

Like her brother.

Like him.

Jack's stomach twisted. It was one thing to live with this thing inside him. Another to think about explaining it to his children. The birds and the bees—and the intergalactic tumor.

Would Max even get to be a teenager before the growth inside him activated? Would Molly? Maybe she'd be spared. Most women never achieved orgasm anyway, right? That thought made Jack want to vomit.

He leaned back in his chair, loosening his tie, rubbing the swell of his belly. It looked like the start of a beer gut. But he knew better. It was the cost of losing control. The last time Megan had begged for intimacy, he'd tried. He almost made it. But it had been too intense, and he'd caved.

Six months. That was how long he'd kept himself locked down since. Megan was patient, but the walls were closing in at home. The tension was thick, unspoken. Constant. Not to mention the never-ending raw erections.

The intercom buzzed.

"Sir?"

Jack blinked. "Yes, Mabel?"

"Your 11:30 is here—Miss Sparrow. And your wife is on line two."

He sighed, shuffling the papers into an organized fashion. "Okay. Put Megan through. And send Miss Sparrow in once I'm off."

He picked up the phone, tossing a handful of the papers into a box behind his desk, then greeted his wife. "Hi, hon. Everything okay?"

"Just wondering if you're coming home for lunch today?" There was a subtle sigh at the end which made him cringe.

"I don't think so. Got a client meeting that might run late." He dismissed her, trying to avoid the pit opening in his stomach.

"Should I bring you something?"

"Nah. I'll grab a bite next door. But hey, can you remind Max about the movie this weekend?"

"Sure. I'll tell him when he gets home."

"Wait—he's not there?"

"He went to the park with the neighbors. Molly too. I'm alone."

He swallowed hard. Alone? Waiting for him to come home?

"Uh, okay, thanks. I've got someone waiting. I've gotta run, I'll talk to you later." He hung up and stared at the receiver for a long second before the door opened.

Mabel escorted Abigail Sparrow inside. Jack stood to greet her.

"Miss Sparrow, always a pleasure. I swear, you look younger every time I see you. Do Faluns age in reverse?"

She smiled, blushing just enough to make her glow. "Aren't you sweet," she said with a smile. "Maybe it's the Earth sun. It's good for the skin."

Jack pulled out a chair and waited while she slipped into it. It always amazed him—out of all the alien species he'd met, the Faluns were the most human-like. In fact, Miss Sparrow herself had once told him they were virtually identical except for minor variations in their DNA—and the fins on their backs. But one rarely saw those unless they were on the beach.

Miss Sparrow had brought a lot of business to Jack over the last couple of years. In fact, she was now his biggest client. Luckily for him, she was pretty plain Jane and professional. Not the type to tempt him. Still, he wasn't blind. The woman had great legs. He noticed. He just didn't linger.

He sat back down. "So... what can I do for you today, Miss Sparrow?"

PART IX – THE BIRDS AND THE BEES

Six years later.

"Jack, you're so funny. So charming, really." Miss Sparrow tucked a strand of hair behind her ear, her voice honey-sweet. "I know it's only been six months, but... when you're ready to start dating, let me know."

Jack raised an eyebrow. "What do you mean?"

She slipped some papers into her bag. "I could set you up with a friend or..." She stood slowly, the curve of her smile calculated. "...or something."

He shifted awkwardly. "Oh, um, yeah. Even though Megan has Katie, I still have Max and Molly. Between work and them, I don't really have time to date right now."

Her smile didn't falter. "Well... if things change."

"Sure." Jack walked her to the door. "It was good seeing you again, Miss Sparrow."

She stopped in the doorway, leaned just a little too close. "Please, Jack... I've told you before." Her voice dropped to a purr. "You can call me Abby."

He looked down, attempting to avoid the look in her eyes—and immediately regretted it. The V-cut of her blouse revealed more than he expected. When had she started dressing like this? Had she always looked this good? Had she had work done?

His brain spiraled. A million questions. None of them safe.

"Jack?"

He blinked, jerking his gaze back up.

Abby let out a slow, knowing laugh, and his cheeks flushed with heat. "Call me when the papers are ready."

"Y-yeah. Shouldn't be more than a week."

She left. Jack closed the door and went straight for the bottom drawer of his desk. The half-full bottle of scotch inside greeted him like an old friend. He poured two fingers and took a long sip. The burn was good. Grounding.

And mercifully, the erection faded.

Maybe it was time to pass Abby—Miss Sparrow—off to Henderson.

His thoughts drifted. Not to work. Not to the growing thing inside him.

To Max.

Ten years old next week. Jack had promised they'd go fishing. But what he hadn't promised—what he was still dreading—was the talk.

The one no father should ever have to give.

How do you explain sex to your child when it comes with a kill switch?

How do you say: *Son, one day your body will betray you. You'll feel urges. And if you act on them… it'll kill you.*

Jack stared into his glass. He took another drink. It didn't help.

Megan would've handled this better. She had a way of softening hard truths. She'd probably sit Max down, draw some stupid diagram, make it into a lesson. Something he could absorb without fear. Without shame.

But this was his fault and his responsibility. The understandable reason the pair lived with him full time and not their mother.

He sighed and finished the glass. The more he tried to hold it all together—for the kids, for work—the more he slipped. Self-control wasn't discipline anymore. It was survival.

He'd need to stop by the liquor store tonight.

PART X – COUNTDOWN

Jack hung up and let his hands rest on his belly. It no longer resembled a beer gut—it had shape now. Round. Tight. Like he'd swallowed a basketball.

That's what you get from late-night Skinemax and too much scotch, he thought.

By the time Megan left him, he'd hit number six. Two more came after too many drinks and a shame spiral. Then came number nine—the result of a regrettable back-alley encounter with a prostitute who smelled like lilacs and whiskey.

Number ten, though? That was the endgame.

Dr. Jones had told him: ten meant viability. Birthing potential. Alien fetus locked and loaded. Whatever the hell that would mean.

So Jack made a decision.

Two days later, he stood in the back corner of Mic & Mac's Sex Emporium, holding what looked like a medieval torture device in polished chrome and black leather.

"That's our best model," the clerk chirped, far too cheerful for someone discussing genital imprisonment. "Steel cage, triple lock, internal curve to redirect any natural excitement. Great for long-term denial or behavioral reinforcement."

Jack nodded absently. The device felt heavier than it should've. Heavier than the dread it was meant to contain.

––––––

At home, it took him three tries, a small amount of petroleum jelly, and a full-blown existential crisis to get the damn thing on. By the end, he was sweating, red-faced, and questioning every life choice that had led him to this moment.

When he clicked the final lock shut, a strange calm fell over him. For the first time in weeks, the countdown paused. Like the final girl in a horror movie who finds the closet door and wedges it shut.

He dropped the key into a padded envelope, addressed to Megan. No return address. No explanation.

She'd get it in a day or two. And once a week, she would mail it back—just long enough for him to clean up, curse his anatomy, and re-cage the beast.

It wasn't a cure.

But it was control.

And right now, control was the closest thing to hope he had left.

At the very least, he wanted to make it until the kids turned eighteen. Sometimes, he swore the universe had other plans—but he tried not to let the weight of that crush him.

Two months into his self-imposed lockdown, he found out just how hard the universe was working against him.

PART XI – ON THE SPOT

The door to his office swung open and Mabel hobbled in, escorting Abigail Sparrow.

Or was it?

"Abby?" Jack stood, hitting his knee on the underside of his desk in his rush to greet the woman. His eyes bounced from head to toe—something was different. Very different.

"Hi, Jack." She smiled like a woman who knew exactly what effect she had. "You look cute when you're speechless." There was something almost too smooth about her voice—like it had been practiced, tuned to hit a frequency Jack didn't know he responded to. But he did.

He blinked. "You're not Abigail—you've got to be her daughter," he said, marveling at the transformation.

"No, it's me," she purred, "but you get points for that comment. I just bought a new wardrobe. Sometimes a shopping spree on the strip can do wonders for a woman—outside and in. That's the thing I love about this planet."

Her golden hair fanned out as she spun, handing her coat to Mabel and showing off a tight blue skirt and revealing white blouse. "What do you think?"

His cheeks flushed as the chastity cage dug in sharply. Jack shifted his stance. It was like his libido had staged a jailbreak and was looking for bolt cutters.

"Fabulous, Abby. Shopping suits you well," he managed.

"Thank you, Jack. I hoped you might like it."

His cheeks reddened at that. Why would she think he would like it?

The door closed behind Mabel with a heavy click, sealing them in silence.

Jack shuffled his feet beneath the desk, doing his best to keep his eyes anywhere but on Abby. But they kept drifting back.

After discussing business for a few minutes, her smile seemed timid as she changed the subject. "Jack, do you like me?"

He hesitated as his mind scrambled at this line of questioning. "Yes... Abby, I do. Of course!"

"Would you maybe like to go out to dinner sometime?" Her voice dipped. "No pressure for anything else—I'd just enjoy your company."

A million thoughts crowded Jack's mind—none of them safe. But he had his cage to protect him. He'd just have to make sure Megan kept the key this week. He exhaled slowly and surrendered. "Sure. I'd like that."

Her face lit up. "Great, Jack. What would you say to dinner at my place? I'll treat you to a fabulous Falun meal—it'll be, well... out of this world."

His mouth opened. Then closed. He crossed his arms and cleared his throat.

"Uhmmm. Your place?" he squeaked.

Gulp.

PART XII – DINNER FOR 3?

Klink.

"To Falun cooking," Jack said as their glasses met.

"To good company," Abby replied, raising her wine with a smile that felt... deliberately seductive.

They sipped. The wine was full-bodied, red, and dangerously smooth. Jack had brought it thinking it would pair well with seafood. Now it tasted like temptation.

"I'm glad you enjoyed it," she said, eyes watching him over the rim of her glass.

"It was delicious," Jack replied, forcing a casual smile. Across the table, Abby's black dress clung to her in ways that seemed sculpted, not sewn. He looked away—then back too quickly. The metal cage pinched as he shifted in his seat.

Thank god for that, he thought. Otherwise I'd be in serious trouble. Or worse.

Eyes locked, the silence that followed wasn't awkward. It was... loaded. He broke it.

"Your eyes," he said. "They're intense. That blue liner—it really makes them pop."

"Thank you," she said, looking down just long enough to seem shy. But when she looked back up, her gaze held his.

"They're kind of... mesmerizing," he added, instantly regretting it.

Abby giggled softly, rising with a feline stretch. The dress moved like liquid. She picked up her glass and motioned to the couch.

"Come. Let's relax."

Jack stood on shaky legs, hand trembling as he picked up his own glass. He reached down, subtly adjusting the cage. Still there. Still locked. As if the pain it was causing him wasn't reminder enough, he needed to make sure it was real. He felt almost lightheaded with desire.

In the living room, Abby sat dead center on the couch, forcing him to choose. He picked the left cushion, seeing half a cheek's more space to keep between them.

"How'd you like the wine?" he asked as he sat.

"It's great. Honestly, good wine's one of the few things keeping me tethered to Earth. That, and good company?" she teased.

He muttered unintelligibly, taking great interest in the fibers of her carpet.

"Would you like more?"

Jack started to rise. "Sure, I'll—"

But her hand landed gently on his knee. Not possessive. Just... deciding.

"I've got it," she said. Her touch lingered an extra beat before she gave a soft squeeze, stood and took his glass.

She walked slowly toward the kitchen. At the doorway, she glanced back, catching him watching her. Her smile widened, soft and knowing.

She laughed once, then vanished through the door.

PART XIII – I THINK YOU HAVE SPOTS

Abby bent low as she handed Jack his glass. "Here you go."

"Thanks," he replied, eyes darting away from the show she was offering—but not quick enough for his body to not respond. In the back of his mind, a voice questioned why she was so interested in a man who looked pregnant, but then again... she was an alien. What they might find attractive was beyond his ability to reason.

She clinked his glass, her smile radiant. "To good company."

They sipped. Jack took a long pull, but something caught his tongue—gritty, like sand. He rubbed it against his teeth and glanced at the glass. A faint film clung to the sides, blue and white specks catching the light.

He held it up. "Hmm. What's this?"

Abby leaned closer, plucking it from his hand. "Oh! I must've grabbed the glasses straight from the dishwasher. Sometimes the detergent doesn't rinse properly. Sorry about that."

Her cheeks flushed as she laughed and set both glasses down on the side table. When she turned back, she wore a nervous grin.

"I really like you, Jack," she said, her voice a little breathless.

Jack slid back on the cushion, his gut tightening. The cage pinched.

"Um. Thank you, Abby. I—" he hesitated, watching her eyes—bright, intense, expectant. "I like you too."

She reached out, took his hand in hers, and leaned in. Her lips met his, soft, gentle, but insistent.

His stayed firm. Still resisting.

She pulled back slowly. "Jack... I'm sorry. Was I too forward?" Her voice cracked. "Am I not—"

"No. No, it's nothing like that." He grabbed her hand as she started to turn away.

"Then what?" she asked, eyes glassy. "Is it because I'm alien?"

Jack winced. "It's not you. It's not even that you're alien. It's—" he stopped himself, his voice catching in his throat. "It's complicated."

Abby tried to laugh, but it came out twisted. "Well, you're gonna give a girl a complex." She turned her head, wiping at the corners of her eyes before she faced him again, her smile trembling.

Jack stared at her for a long moment. She was kind. Beautiful. Patient.

And he was lying to her. The guilt ate at him.

"Look, Abby," he said, his voice low, reaching out to touch her hand. "You deserve the truth."

He told her.

Everything. Mostly.

The Vulgarian deal gone bad. The abduction. The probing. The implant. The pregnancies. The divorce. Everything but the cage—the humiliation of that was too much to share with anyone else. Megan was bad enough, but she had watched his downward spiral first hand.

When he finished, the room fell into silence. Heavy. Dense.

She said nothing for a full minute, but her lips slowly spread into the widest smile.

PART XIV – THE LAST TANGO

"So," she leaned forward, breasts pressing together. Jack's eyes followed the line of cleavage before jerking away. "You mean if you fuck me," she glanced downward with feigned innocence, "you'll die?"

"Y-yes." He averted his eyes to a small scuff mark on the wall. "I should go."

"No, Jack, please don't." She sat back, her tone soft. "I'm sorry if I made you feel awkward. I just… I have to know—have you ever thought about how you'd want it to happen? You know… the last time?"

He gave a nervous laugh. "A little." He met her eyes just long enough to see her grin before retreating back to the floor. "I've lived out a few of my fantasies already. Six and nine—both with," he blushed furiously, "professionals. Expensive, but worth it. I figured if I only had a few chances left, I might as well make them count. Well, that last one wasn't exactly what I'd planned, but…"

Her grin widened. "You're so honest, Jack. I really like that. Most men would never admit something like that."

He looked up at her, cheeks flushed, and managed a nervous smile. "Thank you… I think."

She leaned closer, voice conspiratorial. "So what about the last one? Gonna jerk off into the void, or go out with a bang?"

He coughed, face brightening even further. "I guess... something simple. A woman on top, maybe. Watch her sway. Or maybe just... a long, slow blow job."

"Oooh." She shaped her lips into a perfect 'O' and pushed her tongue into her cheek. "Do you think I could be the girl to give you that last wish?"

Jack's smile vanished. "What?" He tried to sit up but found his body sluggish.

At the same time, Abby straightened and reached for her shoulders. Her dress slipped effortlessly down her arms, revealing full, perfect breasts. The flirtation in her eyes was gone. In its place: hunger.

"I've always wanted a guy who'd die to fuck me," she said, voice low and steady.

"Wh-what?" Jack stammered, fully paralyzed. Her body was beautiful, impossible—and suddenly, terrifying.

She slid to her knees and reached for his waistband.

Jack scrambled back on the couch as if there was somewhere to go, as if his muscles were actually working. He protested. "No, Abby, wait—"

"C'mon, Jack," she cooed. "Let me have it."

"I want to, but I can't—"

"Sure you can, baby." Her voice dripped with amusement. "I'll just open up and say ahhh... or maybe you're into roleplay. We can play army—you lie down and I'll blow you to hell."

He was panting now, unsure whether to laugh or scream. "That's not it!"

Abby yanked and his pants slid down to his knees.

She paused. "What the fuck is that?"

As if his face could get any redder, Jack swallowed hard. He had told her almost everything, but not about that.

"It's called a male chastity belt. I call it protection from myself."

Abby's grin turned sharp. Something behind her eyes flickered— cool and clinical.

"Well, fuck that," she muttered.

She reached down and grabbed it, examining the hardware. "Three locks?" she teased. "Someone's serious."

Snap. The first one popped free as she twisted the metal effortlessly. Jack flinched.

Snap. The second followed, broken, worthless metal.

"You better stop," he gasped. "Abby, please. You don't understand what this means."

Her smile didn't budge. "Oh, Jack," she purred. "I understand perfectly."

She held the third lock between her fingers. "You're not the only one with something inside them dying to get out."

Snap. The third lock broke.

"That baby's mine."

PART XV – THE CLIMAX

Seeing the crumpled locks on the floor, Jack realized two things: one, Faluns were much stronger than they looked— and two, he was fucked. Literally. The restraint that had kept him alive up until now lay in pieces, and his freed erection pointed like a weapon toward the woman who had just dismantled his defenses with a red-lipped smile.

"Oh, look. You've already started." Abby licked the glistening fluid from his tip, never breaking eye contact.

Jack gripped the couch cushion, knuckles white. "Abby—please— don't."

Her voice was flat now. Purposeful. "It's too late, Jack. You're mine."

She took him into her mouth, making him disappear, and with a low hum, so did his objections. Her head moved slowly, methodically. She surfaced with a pop, lips wet and smiling.

"Looks like the Vulgarians are going to be daddies tonight."

She disappeared down again, the humming returning like a vibration through his spine. It wasn't music. It was a ritual. And she was playing him like a sacred instrument.

Somewhere inside, Jack's willpower collapsed under the weight of pleasure and pressure. She pressed down to the curly hairs at the base of his shaft and he groaned.

"The humming," he gasped, "what is that?"

Sliding up with maddening slowness, she stroked him with one hand and slipped the other beneath his balls.

"The Vulgarian birth ritual tones," she said.

Before he could react—to run—his mind screamed. She was back on him—faster, deeper—and then he felt it: a finger slipping inside.

Jack's body jerked up. He tried to pull away. "Wait—hey, I know some guys like that, but I—"

Her free hand snapped up to his shoulder and forced him to stay in place, her supernatural strength not even needed to stop his resistance. His voice dissolved into a moan. She didn't stop. The finger didn't stop. It slid deeper than it should've, snaking its way up, up, up.

"Oh fuck—ohhhh fuuuck!"

The orgasm ripped through him like a shuddering collapse. He cried out as he came, trembling, the world narrowing to Abby's mouth and the consuming pressure behind his eyes.

She swallowed everything. If he could've seen what she consumed, he might've vomited. The fluid was thick—green like snot, streaked with red. But she smiled as she slurped off him and pulled her finger out like it was the final note of a decadent meal.

Jack collapsed back, gasping, sweat cooling on his forehead.

When his vision steadied, he looked down.

Abby held her hand in front of her face, the middle finger elongated—twelve inches of glistening, bloodied alien anatomy. The nail itself was an inch long and thin like a razor. The whole thing was covered in blood and goo.

"What the hell did you do?"

She smiled, eyes gleaming. Without breaking eye contact, she slipped the finger into her mouth and moaned as she sucked it clean. When she pulled it out, it had returned to human proportions.

"That," she said in a raspy purr, "was wonderful, Jack. There is nothing quite like the taste of Vulgarian gestational fluid at the moment of fertilization."

Jack tried to sit up. "What did you do to me?"

She leaned forward, resting her head gently on his bulging belly. Her voice was tender now, almost reverent.

"Let me tell you, Jack…"

PART XVI – THE REST OF THE STORY

"The Vulgarian fetus has to be fertilized by a female Falun in order to achieve birth."

"What?" Jack sat up, then collapsed back down as his belly gurgled and twisted beneath the surface. His head spun. "You fertilized the fetus?"

"Yes."

"But I thought it fed on some chemical released during orgasm?" Jack's chest heaved. Panic was overtaking reason.

"Oh, it does," she said, slipping the straps of her dress back over her shoulders, her voice casual—clinical. "But it needs a little help to come to fruition."

Jack's brow furrowed, confusion sliding into dread. "But that means... what would've happened if—"

Abby's eyes flashed. The dark lines beneath them pulsed against the radiant flare of her pupils.

"You mean if I hadn't been here for your tenth orgasm?"

She looked down, smoothing the hem of her dress like they were discussing nothing more than the weather.

He nodded slowly, as the dawning realization set in.

"The fetus would've entered a dormant gestation period. After forty-eight hours, if fertilization did not occur, your body would've aborted it. And the cycle would have started again."

Jack stared, mouth dry, eyes wide. "You mean… I could've lived? I could've had a sex life? I could've stayed with my wife?"

He meant to wield the words like a bludgeon, each one heavier than the last.

Abby didn't blink. "Probably."

It wasn't cruelty. It was indifference.

That made it worse.

Jack lurched upright. "I have to tell Max and Molly. They can still live normal lives. They can have futures!"

He tried to rise, but the stars dancing in his vision doubled, then tripled. His body failed him.

Abby placed a hand on his chest and pushed.

"You're not going anywhere, Jack. And when the time comes," she said, leaning close, her breath cold against his cheek, "I'll be there for both Max and Molly."

"No…" Jack gasped, hand pressing to the mound of his gut. The gurgling within had grown louder. Constant. "You can't… you can't get them both."

Abby tilted her head, then let a slow sneer spread across her face. "Why not? Am I not pretty enough?"

Before he could answer—not that it mattered—her form shimmered and restructured. In place of the woman stood a handsome young man, familiar in the worst way.

A client.

Jack's stomach turned again.

"Whichever way they swing," Abby said with a wink, her voice now masculine and smooth, "I'll be ready to play."

"You're a shapeshifter?" Jack whispered, the last of his strength draining from the question.

"Uh, duh." The man smirked, then transformed back to Abby—glowing, radiant, monstrous.

"Now sit back," she said, her voice low and reverent. "I know you feel it moving. It doesn't hurt yet—there aren't enough nerve endings inside. But once it begins to push up?"

She ran a finger down his cheek.

"I've been told my beauty helps ease the pain." She pressed her shoulders together, pushing the swell of her breasts to their maximum.

A shape pressed against the inside of Jack's stomach. A bony, reptilian hand stretching the skin outward like a latex glove pulled too tight, straining toward rupture.

Abby's face swelled with pride, and her true form revealed.

Jack screamed.

EPILOGUE: F.I.F.O.

Fifteen minutes later.

A knock on the door.

Abby opened it, a small bundle swaddled in a blanket in her arms. Something within it gurgled, wet and rhythmic. She slipped a finger between its gums, and the infant latched with a greedy squeal.

She looked up at the figure in the doorway—hulking, wet-eyed, and smiling.

"Whose... is... it?" Edgar croaked, his voice thick with anticipation.

Abby smiled, eyes glittering.

"He's got your jowls, Commander. First in..." she trailed off, offering the bundle into his waiting arms, "...first out."

Edgar held the infant Vulgarian close, its pale skin mottled with green veins. One tiny hand reached up, clawed and twitching. Edgar grinned, a long string of saliva stretching from his lip.

"Rank... has... privileges."

"The first of many," she whispered, more to the bundle than to him.

———

AFTERWORD

Dear Reader,

Thanks for joining me for this bizarro sci-fi adventure! I hope you enjoyed it.

If you did, you might also like my Horror Anthology, Mashed: The Culinary Delights of Twisted Erotic Horror.

MASHED is what happens when your favorite cooking show collides with *The Twilight Zone*—and then gets dragged into a back alley by a horny demon, a killer baker, and a sentient slab of meat.

You can grab a copy on Amazon at myBook.to/mashed!

And for those of you sticking around for more, I have a special treat! A free preview of the first book in my comedy zombie series, The Zee Brothers: Curse of the Zombie Omelet!

-Grivante

P.S. 💀 **Loved F.I.F.O.?** Your review helps summon the next horror!

If *F.I.F.O.* left you laughing, cringing, or questioning your life choices in the best way possible—**please consider leaving a 5-star review!**

Your feedback helps us serve up more depraved delights to horror lovers like you. 😈

ABOUT THE AUTHOR

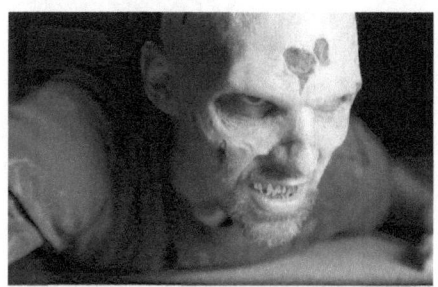

Grivante, pronounced "Gri-von-tay", enjoys writing humorous and bizarre fiction. He hopes you laugh as much reading his works as he does writing them.

Visit www.grivantepress.com or the social media links below to find more by this author!

BB bookbub.com/authors/grivante
f   facebook.com/grivante
X   x.com/grivante
⊙   instagram.com/grivante

THE ZEE BROTHERS VOL.1
PREVIEW

PART I - MR. PEMBLETON

"'m sorry sir, it doesn't appear to be a rodent problem."

"What do you mean? Not rodents? All that scratching and scurrying all night long? What type of bugs can be making that kind of racket?"

The man from the pest control company looked down and rubbed his name tag, which read 'Burt', with his right hand. "Sir, do you know if this area may have once been home to a graveyard?"

Mr. Pembleton's brow furrowed. What kind of question was that? "Well, yeah, this whole area was once Pakatini tribal lands. My neighbor Shirley told me there are small family buried plots all over. Just last week, the Hembrooks over on Lancaster, dug up a pile of bones and some kind of am-let thingy. They threw it all out in the trash. Bones in their back yard. Can you believe it?"

Mr. Pembleton stopped there, a sparkle of realization dawning. "Wait, are you trying to tell me there are bones down there and a dog or some feral cat got in 'em?"

Burt's eyes widened at that. "Um, no Sir. From the way the earth is disturbed and the scratch marks on the floor joists and foundation, I would say you have a zombie infestation."

Mr. Pembleton blinked twice. He rubbed his grey and black

whiskered jaw and adjusted his false teeth, then asked, "How much is that gonna cost?"

"I don't know Sir, we don't handle zombies. We only make living things dead, not, um, dead things dead."

"Who does then?"

Burt, sweating a little from his brow, broke his stance and started checking his pockets. "We, uh, technically aren't supposed to recommend anyone, but, um, there are these brothers. They have a little side business and I've got their card here somewhere. With the apocalypse coming there's been more and more of a need for their services." He was now flipping through his wallet, his pockets having revealed nothing but lint and old cough drop wrappers. He ate them constantly to keep the smell of the poisons he used from making his nose itch.

"Which apocalypse is that? Was it that Nostradumbass fella again? He predicted Hitler and the Obamanation of our country, or wait, I saw one on TV the other day that said George Clooney was the anti-Christ and if he sees his reflection in the mirror at the Vatican—"

"Ah," Burt pulled a tattered business card from his wallet and thrust it at Mr. Pembleton, interrupting his rant. "Here you go!"

> *Zee Brothers : Zombie Exterminators*
> *Jonah & Judas : Owner Operators*
> *888-867-5309*
> *Ask for Jenny*
> *"We keep the dead, dead!"*

Burt made his way to the door.

Mr. Pembleton looked up from the card. "Are these guys any good?"

Burt's hand was on the front door knob. "Well, I don't know, Sir. No one I've given their card to has ever called to tell me, I just know they're a bit... different." He twisted the knob and swung the door open.

Mr. Pembleton opened his mouth to speak but Burt spoke first.

"Best of luck Mr. P., no charge for the inspection. Have a Pest Free Day!"

Slam!

Burt scurried down the drive, popping a cough drop into his mouth and breathing in the sweet menthol, never hearing, but knowing exactly what Mr. Pembleton had wanted to ask: "What do you mean, different?"

Inside, Mr. Pembleton's eyes drifted back to the card. He shambled off to find his phone, muttering under his breath. "Different, huh? This better not cost too much."

———

PART II - THE ZEE BROTHERS

R ing!

"Zee Brothers!" a male voice answered. "How can we help you?"

"Uh, yes, is Jenny available?"

Laughter erupted from the other end so loud that even though Mr. Pembleton's hearing wasn't the best, he had to hold the phone away from his ear until it died down.

"This is Judas, Owner, How—, OW!"

There was a clambering and clamoring on the other end for a moment, then a different voice came back on the phone. "This is Jonah, Owner of Zee Brothers, Zombie Exterminators. How can I help you?"

"My name is Larry Pembleton. I live at 547 Westerly Drive, the pest control man just left and he gave me your card. He thinks I might have a zombie infestation."

"Mhm," the voice on the other end responded. "Just a minute, Mr. Pembleton."

For a moment all Mr. Pembleton could hear were muffled voices as it sounded like someone had placed their hand over the receiver.

"Sir," the second voice came back on the line, "Ok, what else can you tell me?"

"Well, Burt asked if the house was built over any kind of cemetery."

"And is it?"

"Well, yes, yes, it is. Most of this development was built over the old Pakatini Reservation for the new county dump and our fabulous gated community of Winter Oaks. Progress, you know. The Pakatinis all died off years ago."

"And you said Burt? From Pests B' Gone?"

"Yeah, that's what his tag said." Mr. Pembleton was getting annoyed. "Look mister, how much is this going to cost?"

"Mr. Pembleton, I need you to listen really closely to me. The infestation, is it in the crawl space under your house?"

"Why, does that cost extra?"

"No. Look, it's almost sundown. I need you to go and make sure that Burt closed and locked the cover to your crawl space."

"Alright, alright," Mr. Pembleton grumbled as he got up out of his chair. "But seriously, how much is this going to cost me?" He shuffled off down the hall to the closet.

Behind the closed door, the hatch to the crawlspace was indeed open. A skeletal hand of bone and decayed flesh fumbled around, looking for leverage to lift itself.

"We'll talk price in a minute Mr. Pembleton. Let's just make sure that thing is locked up tight for now. These native zombie types generally only rise after sundown and they're usually searching for, or upset about, something. Can you tell me if you've been doing any yard work lately and maybe disturbed some bones?"

Mr. Pembleton came to a stop just outside the closet door. "Now listen here, mister. I don't know what kind of negotiation tactics you're playing at, but all these games ain't gonna make me do anything more till you give me a price! And I ain't done no landscaping, it was the Hembrooks over on Lancaster. If they were the ones that caused this, then they the ones that need to be paying for it! I don't care if he's president of the Homeowners' Association and what not!!" Mr Pembleton was full on shouting now, his hand resting on the knob and he pulled the door open.

"I keep my grass cut, just like it says in our covenants and if he up and disturbed some kind of zombie omelet he's gonna pay!"

"Zombie omelet?" Jonah asked.

"Ahhhhh!"

Mr. Pembleton fell over backwards, more in fright then from the weight of the small frame lunging at him. The phone fell from his grasp and his screams were soon replaced by the rending of flesh and gurgling of blood.

Then a low guttural moan, "Ommmmllet."

His brother raised his eyebrows as he watched him. "Well? We got a customer or not?"

Jonah sighed, his lips flapping as he did so. "No, I'm pretty sure he just died."

"What!? I knew you shoulda let me talk to him!" Judas's head bounced with each word, spit flying.

Jonah glared at his brother. "Burt left the crawl space open when he left."

"Burt from Pests B' Gone?"

"Yeah. That Burt."

"Well, shit. What we gonna do now, Jonah?"

Jonah shook his head, "Load up Sasha. We're gonna have to go clean this up before it gets outta hand."

Judas stood, grabbing a shotgun from the couch next to him. "Wait a minute. What was that about a zombie omelet? Did that guy have some sort of weird cannibal fetish?"

Jonah shrugged. "I've no idea, but don't forget to feed Fido before we go."

———

Find out what happens next in, The Zee Brothers: Curse of the Zombie Omelet! At myBook.to/zxseries

www.ingramcontent.com/pod-product-compliance
Lightning Source LLC
Chambersburg PA
CBHW020557130626
46552CB00007B/2928